Enchanted Tree

DAVY LIU

For the Creator

Grateful acknowledgement
to Dr. Mark Arvidson and Laura Derico
for their creative input and insight.

Enchanted Tree
ISBN: 9781937212254
Updated Edition - First Printing: July 2016
Published by Green Egg Media, Inc.
Irvine, California
greeneggmediagroup.com

Text and Illustrations copyright 2012 and 2016 by
Kendu Films, LLC. California
kendufilms.com

Printed in Korea through Codra Enterprises, Inc.
codra.com

Long ago, there was a paradise garden.
It was beautiful and good in every way.

Each creature that lived in this garden was made
to be different.

Miki was a graceful tomboy, swinging in the trees.

Reina thought she was a queen, with her tall, feathery
crown.

Leona was strong and quiet. She kept her spotted coat
tidy and smooth.

Then there was Octavia.

Octavia had a funny-shaped mouth. She had short, stubby legs. She had webbed toes, sharp claws, and a flat tail.

Everyone thought Octavia was odd.

Even Octavia.

One day, the animals were joking and teasing Octavia.
Suddenly, they heard the swoop of giant wings.

The animals stared. What was that in the sky?

The creature landed close by.

"Hello, friends." The stranger spoke with a golden voice. "I am Sunbird."

"Where are you from?" asked Reina.

"I have come from everywhere. I have seen everything. And I have come to you now to share my secrets."

Sunbird told them about an enchanted tree that grew in the center of the paradise garden.

"If you eat this tree's special fruit, you can become like me. You can change. You can be anything you want to be," Sunbird promised.

Her words sounded good. All the animals wanted to taste this fruit.

But Octavia wanted it most of all. Octavia wanted to be beautiful like the other animals.

Just then, the animals heard a strange sound.
Before they could ask Sunbird any more questions,
she flew away over the trees.

The sound grew louder. It was footsteps!

Another odd creature appeared in the garden. This
one had no feathers or fur. He had no scales or spots.
He was a two-feeter.

The animals had never seen anything like him. Octavia
and the others followed him all the way to his nest.

"The poor two-feeter is all alone," Leona said.

Miki had an idea. "Let's grab some fruit and take it to him. Maybe that will make him happy!"

And that is what they did. Soon every animal in the garden was the two-feeter's friend.

He gave each animal a name.

He called Reina "crane."

He called Miki "lemur."

And he called Leona "leopard."

When he came to Octavia, he thought for a long time. Finally, he smiled and said, "Platypus!"

The animals liked being friends with the two-feeter. But they could see he was still lonely. There were no other creatures like him in the entire garden.

The animals tried to make their friend laugh.

Miki swung in huge loops with her long tail.

Leona jumped up high and thumped down with her heavy paws.

Reina danced on her skinny legs.

Octavia smacked her flat tail on the water, making big splashes.

The two-feeter smiled at his animal friends. But they could see something was missing.

Then one night, an amazing thing happened.
The two-feeter fell into a deep, deep sleep.
As he slept, another two-feeter appeared!

The new two-feeter had beautiful hair and eyelashes.
The animals saw that she was the perfect mate for
their friend.

Sunbird saw the two-feeters too. She saw that they were perfectly happy together. And she was jealous, for she had lied.

It was true that Sunbird could change her shape. But she had not eaten the special fruit from the enchanted tree. And no matter how hard the creature tried, she could not be beautiful like the new two-feeter.

And Sunbird could not be perfectly happy.

So Sunbird made a plan.

She had heard the Maker of the garden warn the two-feeters. The Maker instructed them not to eat from the enchanted tree. All the other fruit was good. But if they ate from that tree, death would enter the garden!

Sunbird said to herself, "I will trick them. I will get them to eat from the enchanted tree!"

While Sunbird planned her trick, Octavia stayed with the beautiful two-feeter. She loved to play in the river with her.

"I wish I could be as beautiful as she is," Octavia said. Just then she remembered the words of Sunbird: "If you eat this tree's special fruit . . . you can change. You can be anything you want to be."

Octavia knew what she had to do. She had to find that tree! As soon as she set off to search for it, Sunbird appeared.

"Bring your friends and follow me," Sunbird said.
"I will lead you to the enchanted tree."
Octavia and the other animals followed Sunbird.

The beautiful two-feeter saw the animals looking at the sky. She followed them to see where they were going.

When they finally reached the enchanted tree, Sunbird's voice called out to them. "Come and see this beautiful tree. Touch its beautiful leaves."

The animals noticed that Sunbird had changed her shape. Now the creature curled herself around a shiny piece of fruit and held it out to the two-feeter. "Eat its beautiful fruit!"

The two-feeter took the fruit in her hand. She looked into Sunbird's eyes. "Such a beautiful creature. And such beautiful fruit! I wonder why the Maker told us not to eat it?"

Sunbird whispered in a voice only the two-feeter could hear, "Ah, but in the Maker's garden, everything that is beautiful is good. Look at you! You are beautiful and good. You can't do anything bad. Just taste the fruit and you will see. It is also beautiful and good."

The two-feeter quickly put the fruit in her mouth. Gulp! She ate it in big bites and reached for more.

Octavia stared at the fruit with wide eyes. She wanted to taste it! But the two-feeter turned away from her friends and ran into the thick woods.

The animals scurried after the two-feeter, all the way back to her nest. There she shared the fruit with her mate.

Octavia felt a strange feeling in her heart.
She was angry.

"Why didn't she share the fruit with us?" the platypus
said.

Octavia looked at her funny reflection in a pool of
water. She became very sad.

"That two-feeter is not my friend!" she said.
The other animals felt angry and sad too.

"Maybe there is still time! Sunbird could give us fruit too! Let's go to the tree!" Octavia waddled as fast as her webbed feet would go back through the woods. The others followed her.

Darkness covered the sky. A chill wind blew through the garden.

Back in the two-feeters' nest, they shivered. They saw that they had nothing on their bodies, and they made coverings for themselves.

They felt a new, sad feeling in their hearts. Suddenly they knew. They had done wrong. They had not followed the Maker's instructions.

They were ashamed.

Back at the tree, Sunbird was still curled around the branches. She was laughing.

"I did it! I tricked them! No more perfect happiness for them! Ha, ha, ha!"

The animals watched as the creature slithered up to the highest branches. She leaped out from the tree, waiting for her wings to appear. But there were no wings, no beautiful feathers.

Sunbird fell with a big THUD!

A voice spoke that only Sunbird could hear.
The Maker said she would now be under a curse.
She could never change shape again. Because of her lies,
Sunbird would crawl on her belly all of her days.

The two-feeters had chosen to believe lies, instead of their Maker. Now they would have to leave the paradise garden.

They would know pain and sorrow. They would work hard all of their days. And their days would come to an end.

They would always long to return to the Maker's garden.

The Maker set a special guard to block the way to the garden and hide it from view. The beautiful and good paradise disappeared.

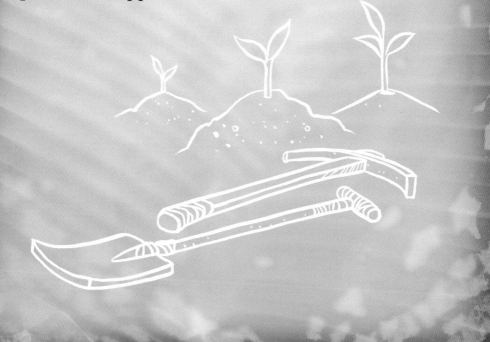

Octavia and the other animals had to work hard to find food.

More two-feeters filled the land. Some of them were good to the animals. Some of them were bad.

Octavia had many platypus babies. When she saw how beautiful they were, she was proud. She didn't want to look different any more. She was glad she had a perfect tail to help her swim and claws to keep her family safe.

The Maker had formed her well.

The Maker no longer walked with them as he did in the garden. But his voice never left them.

The two-feeters and the animals knew the Maker would always watch over them. And someday, the Maker will bring them to a new paradise garden.

All creatures who wish to be made perfectly beautiful and good again will enter that place.

And they will be perfectly happy together.

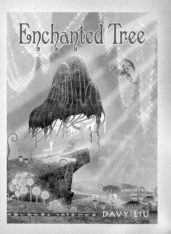

Artist and Author Davy Liu immigrated to the United States at age 13. Within a few months, his talent for drawing and painting was discovered.

At age 19 Davy began a career in feature films working for Disney Studios, Warner Bros and Industrial Light and Magic. His work has appeared in *The Beauty and The Beast, Aladdin, Mulan, The Lion King* and *Star Wars Episode I.*

Every year Davy speaks to over 250,000 people, sharing his inspirational story of overcoming the incredible odds he faced in his youth.

To learn how to draw characters from the Invisible Tails series and to see Davy's speaking schedule, go to InvisibleTails.com